29940
Mole Music

McPhail, David
BL: 2.7
Pts: 0.5   LG

MOLE MUSIC

Henry Holt and Company · New York

MOLE MUSIC

Written and illustrated by
David McPhail

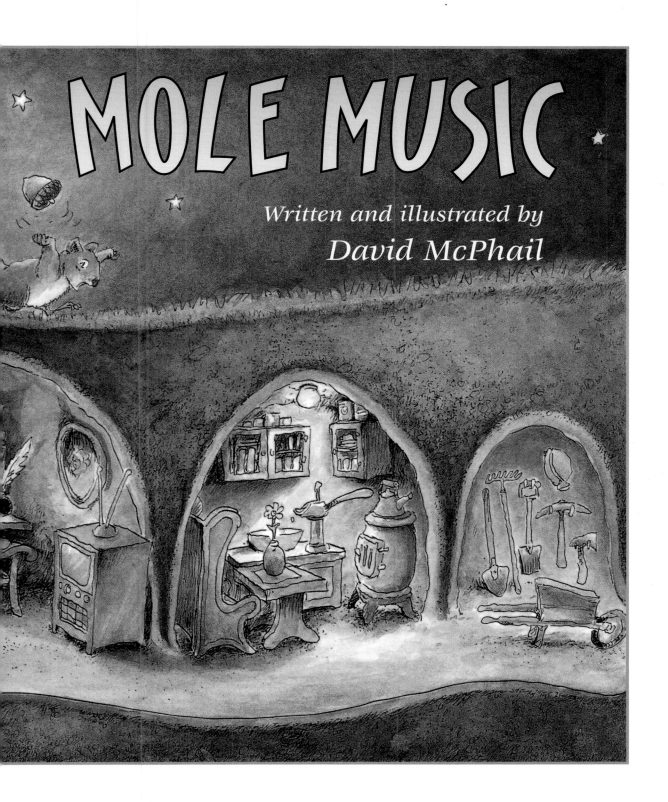

For Lisa,
and for the GANG at SWIFT—
Great job!
and special thanks to Nancy, who made the music possible

Henry Holt and Company, Inc.
Publishers since 1866
115 West 18th Street
New York, New York 10011

Henry Holt is a registered trademark of Henry Holt and Company, Inc.
Copyright © 1999 by David McPhail. All rights reserved.
Published in Canada by Fitzhenry & Whiteside Ltd.,
195 Allstate Parkway, Markham, Ontario L3R 4T8.

Library of Congress Cataloging-in-Publication Data
McPhail, David M.
Mole music/by David McPhail.
Summary: Feeling that something is missing in his simple life,
Mole acquires a violin and learns to make beautiful, joyful music.
[1. Moles (Animals)—Fiction. 2. Violin—Fiction. 3. Music—Fiction.] I. Title.
PZ7.M4788185Mo 1999 [E]—dc21 98-21318

ISBN 0-8050-2819-6 / First Edition—1999
Typography by Martha Rago
The artist used watercolor and ink on illustration board to
create the illustrations for this book.
Printed in the United States of America on acid-free paper.∞
1 3 5 7 9 10 8 6 4 2

Mole lived all alone underground. He spent his days digging tunnels.

At night he ate his supper in front of the
TV and then went to bed.

Mole liked his life, but lately he had begun
to feel there was something missing.

One night on the television a man played the violin. He made the most beautiful music Mole had ever heard.

"I want to make beautiful music, too," Mole said to himself.

So the next day he sent away for a violin
of his own.

Every day Mole checked his mailbox.

No violin.

Finally, after nearly three weeks, it arrived.

Mole was so excited.

He picked up the violin and drew the bow across the strings.

But instead of beautiful music, all he made was a horrible screeching sound.

Mole tried again.

The violin still screeched, but not quite
so horribly.

Mole kept at it.

After about a week he could play one note—
then two. And before a month went by, he
could play an entire scale.

Mole continued to practice.

He learned to put the notes together in a
simple song.

Years went by.

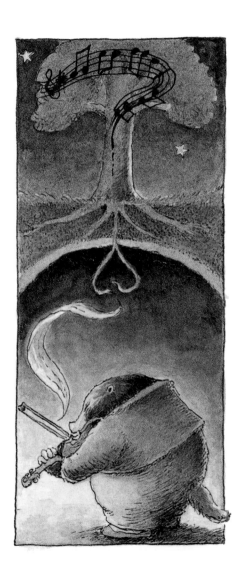 

Mole got better and better.

He was happier than he'd ever been.
During the day, as he dug tunnels,
Mole hummed the music he would
play at night.

Now Mole played even
better than the man he'd
seen on TV so long ago.

Sometimes he wondered
what it would be like to
play his music for people.

He imagined himself playing
before a huge audience.

He imagined that he played
for presidents and queens.

He even imagined that his music could
reach into people's hearts and melt away
their anger and sadness.

Why, maybe his music
could even change the world!

Mole laughed at himself.

"How silly I am," he thought, "imagining that my music could do all that, when no one has ever even heard it."

Mole played one more song,

then put down his violin and went to sleep.
And dreamed beautiful, peaceful dreams.

Fic
McPhail

McPHAIL
Mole music.

JAN 2 5 05	DATE DUE	
NOV 0 7		
DEC 1 6 05		
APR 2 4 06		
MAR 2 9		
MAY 0 2		
MAY 1 6 JAN 3 0		
DEC 0 7		